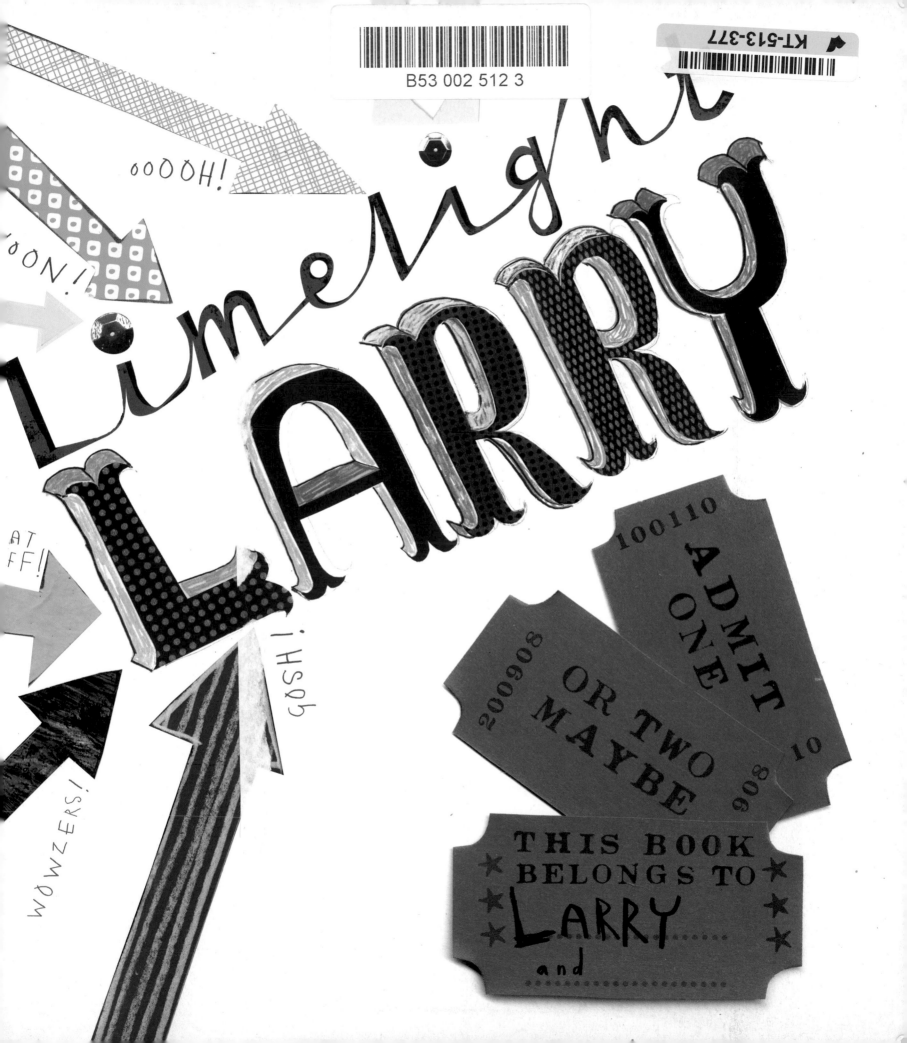

Limelight LARRY

oOOOH!

¡ON!

AT FF!

gosh!

wowzers!

100110

ADMIT ONE

200908

OR TWO MAYBE

10

806

THIS BOOK BELONGS TO

★ LARRY ★ and

ORCHARD BOOKS

338 Euston Road, London NW1 3BH

Orchard Books Australia

Level 17/207 Kent Street, Sydney, NSW 2000

First published in 2010 by Orchard Books

First published in paperback in 2011

ISBN 978 1 40830 184 5

Text and illustrations © Leigh Hodgkinson 2010

The right of Leigh Hodgkinson to be identified as the author and illustrator of this work has been asserted by her in accordance with the Copyrights, Designs and Patents Act, 1988.

A CIP catalogue record for this book is available from the British Library.

2 4 6 8 10 9 7 5 3 1

Printed in China

Orchard Books is a division of Hachette Children's Books, an Hachette UK company.

www.hachette.co.uk

For fun activities and to find out more about Leigh, visit:

www.wonkybutton.com

(handwritten annotations:) LARRY ONLY deaLS with THE BEST · send LARRY FAN MAIL heRE please · YAWN BORING YAWN · Limelight LARRY actually · so tHis Bit means LARRY has tHE copyRigHt RigHt? · I ♡ LARRY · (which IS A division of... um... LIMELIGHT LTD) · oR moRe IMPORTANTLY LimeLight · LARRY

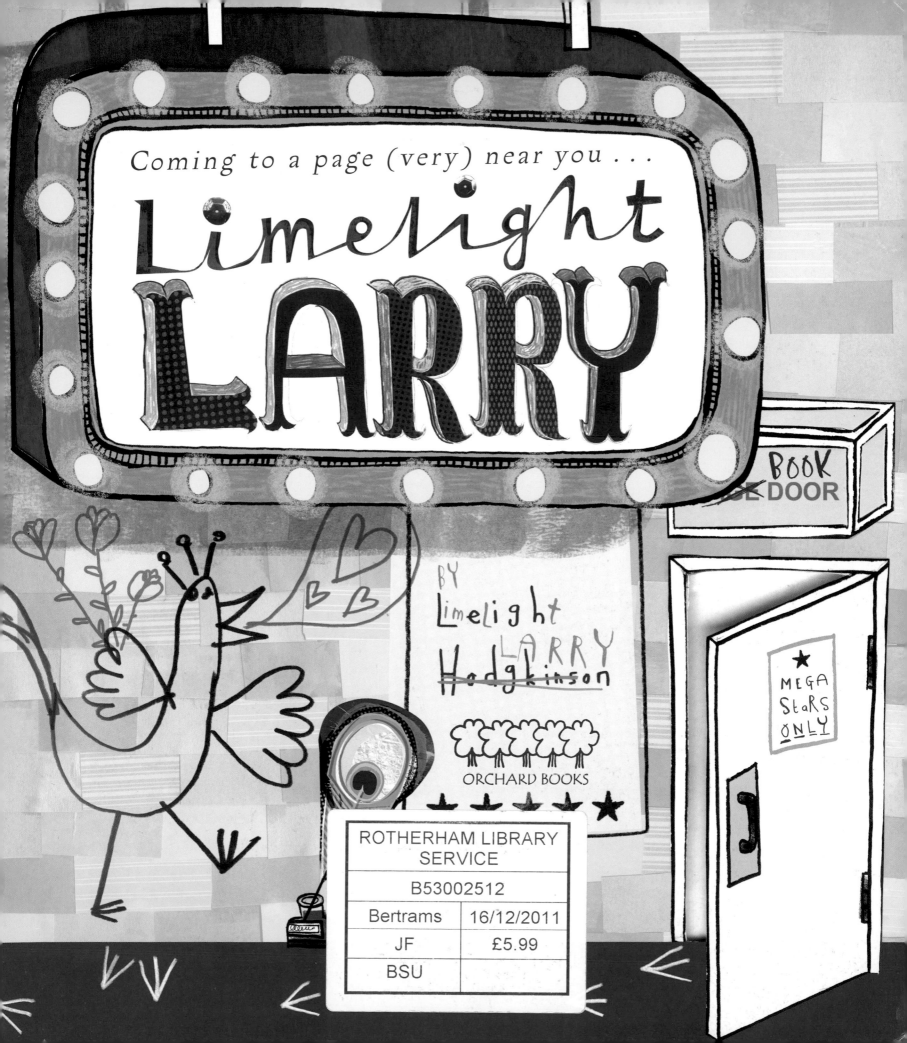

Coming to a page (very) near you . . .

Limelight LARRY

BY Limelight LARRY ~~Hodgkinson~~

ORCHARD BOOKS

BOOK DOOR

MEGA STARS ONLY

YooHoo!

This is Limelight LARRY.

This is a book about him.

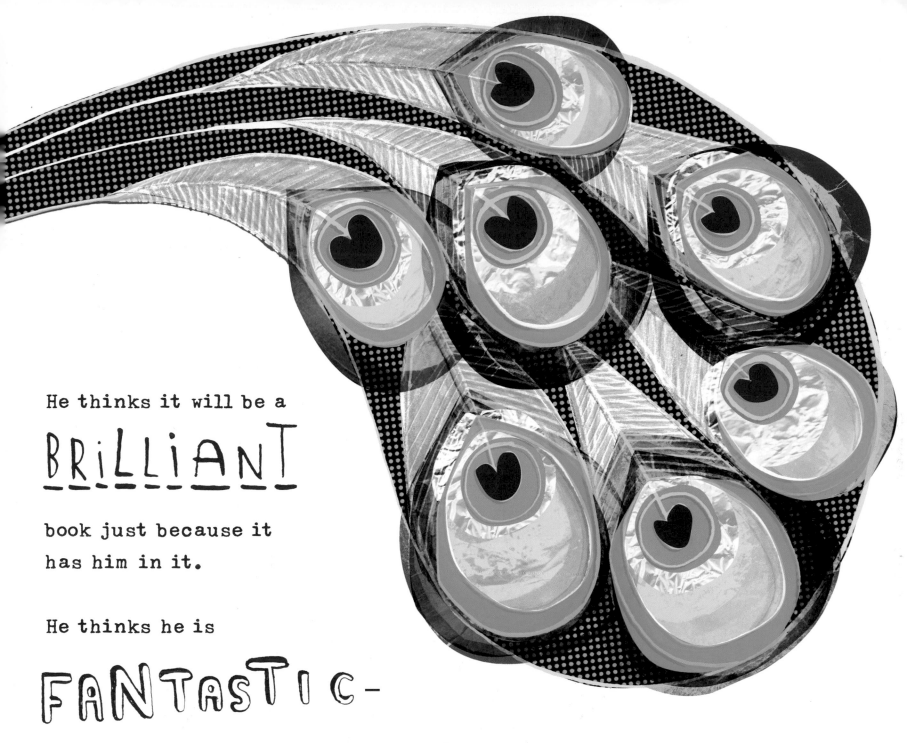

He thinks it will be a

BRiLLiANT

book just because it has him in it.

He thinks he is

FANTasTIC-

the bee's knees with a cherry on top.

He thinks he should be

FAMOUS

and that there should be more books about him.

(Perhaps he should wait and see if this book is any good first, hey?)

SUDDENLY

Limelight Larry spots something out of the corner of his eye . . .

"What do you want, Mouse?"
says Larry to *Mouse*.
"This is a book all about
ME, not **YOU**.

There is NO room for you
on that page.

LOOK! You're making it all

messy!"

"Ooooh!" whispers *Mouse*.
"Is this a book, then?
Does this mean I'm in a real
live book? *Crumbs*."

"Did I hear someone say this is a book?" says Bird,
who has appeared out of nowhere. "Can I be in it?
I could do something funny on the next page,
like hop on one leg for a bit or something."

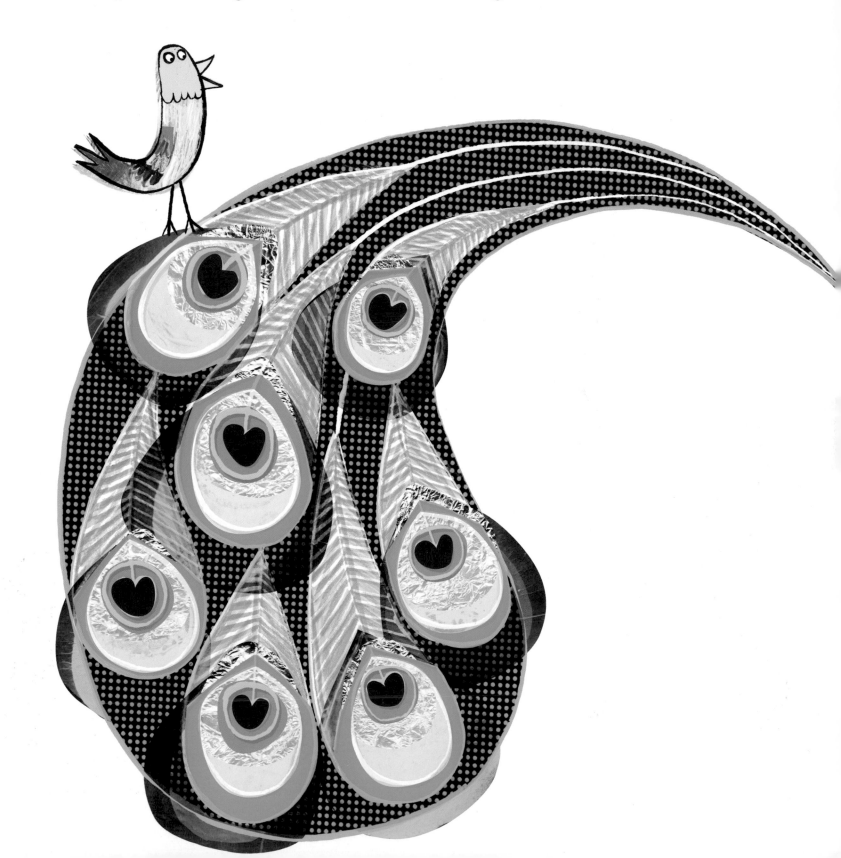

"For your information, YES, this is a book," says Larry.

"But if ANYBODY is going to do anything funny,

or even *slightly* amusing,

it will be

ME!"

LARRY is not too keen on Bird (or anyone) stealing his limelight.

(This book is not called 'Limelight Larry' for nothing, you know.)

It seems that **Elephant** was just in the neighbourhood
and has popped by to see what all the fuss is about.

Mouse tells him EVERYthing
he knows about Larry's book
(which isn't much).

HOP HOPPITY hop

"In MY opinion," booms **Elephant**, "the thing that makes a book interesting is a BIG surprise right at the end."

"Maybe Elephant is the

BIG

surprise,"

suggests *Mouse* helpfully.

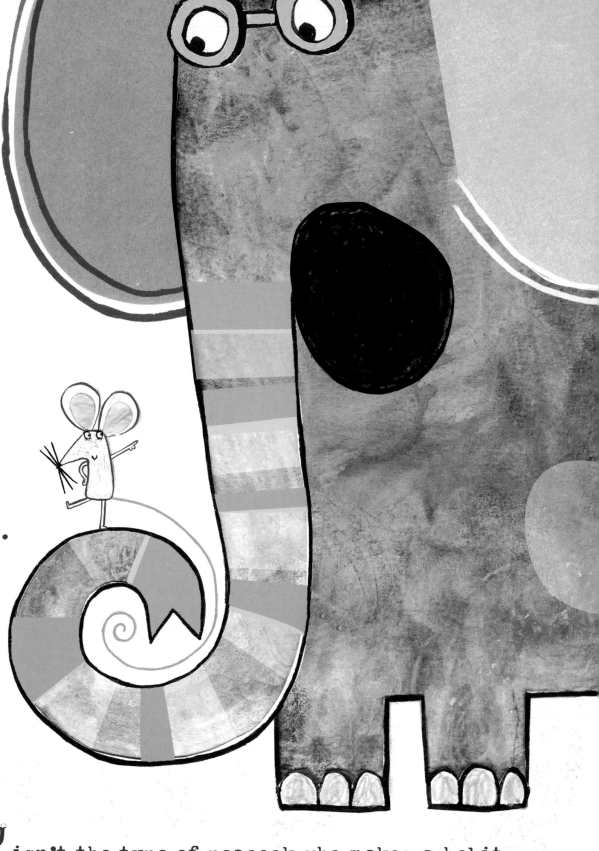

LARRY isn't the type of peacock who makes a habit of listening to the opinions of mice OR elephants. He secretly decides there will be no BIG surprises in THIS book. Besides, it's not anywhere near the end yet.

"Elephant's got a point, Larry," says *Wolf*
(who must have been earwigging from over the page).

"But if you ask me . . .
what every fairy story needs is a good
old-fashioned SCARY wood. It must be your
lucky day as I found this one out the back!"

SNORT!

"Ooh, how very kind of
Wolf," squeals *Mouse*.

LARRY doesn't think so. Larry also doesn't
think the wood is in the least bit scary.
In fact, Larry thinks it's a RUBBISH wood.

PROPS DEPARTMENT

And, by the way, this book is certainly **NOT** a fairy story.

With his snooty beak firmly up in the air, LARRY doesn't even notice that **Bear** has arrived.

(Everybody knows that bears love woodland tea parties.)

Bear looks at his watch. He is hoping that the other tea party guests won't be too late to be in the book.

Mouse wonders if there will be cheesecake.

Wolf hopes there will be fairy cakes.

Bird isn't really interested in tea parties right now . . .

Elephant worries there won't be enough Lemonade to go round . . .

...while LARRY just CAN'T BELIEVE WHAT IS GOING ON!

This whole thing is getting SILLY.

The page is completely cluttered, and Larry's lovely feathers are starting to get all crimpled and crumpled.

This is **NOT** what he had hoped his book would be! Apart from there being

FAR far far FAR far FAR

too many words . . .

Bear is too popular,

Bunny is too cute,

Elephant is too big and clever,

Bird is too funny,

Wolf is too interested in fairy stories

and *Mouse* is too nice and helpful (and has been in too many pages for Larry's liking).

It would be fair to say that

EVERYBODY

is cramping Larry's style!

SLURP

Well, not for long.
Larry decides to make a big, fat, flappy fuss and SCREECHES,

"None of you NIMWITS are even supposed to be here. This is a Limelight LARRY book. If you don't believe me, look on the cover! So take the hint and CLEAR OFF and leave ME and my book ALONE!"

BUT it's far too late for that.
You see, everybody is ALREADY in the book.

Although, as far as Larry's concerned, it's certainly NOT too late. There is only one thing for it . . .

...take up the whole page himself and

SHOW OFF!

BUT

after a while . . .
Larry begins to wonder,
what is the point of showing off on your own?

It's CERTAINLY not much fun.

And, oh dear, the wood seems a lot more SPOOKY and "SCARY"

now that Larry is all ALONE and in the DARK.

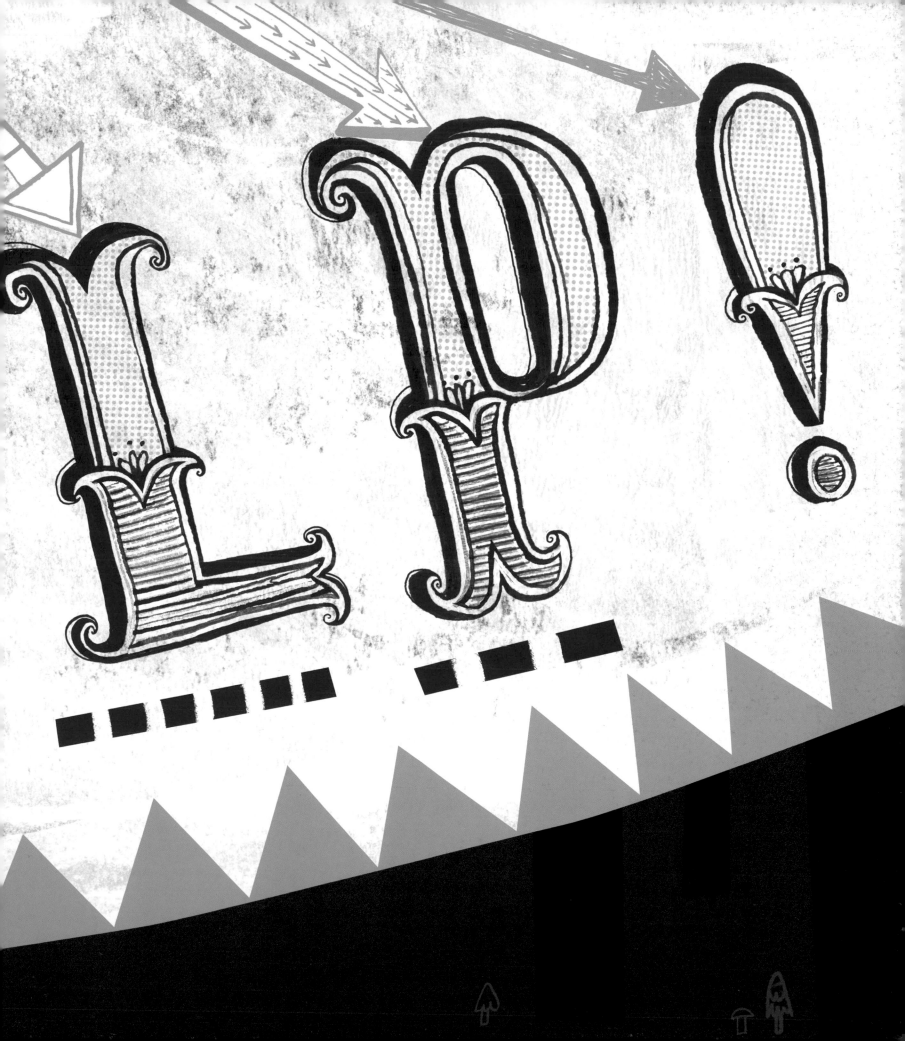

What was that, Larry?

Beg your pardon, Larry?

PLEASE?

Sorry, didn't quite get that, LARRY . . .

Well, it looks as though
Elephant was right.

This book **does** have a
BIG surprise at the end.

But who would have guessed the **BIG** surprise is . . .

... Limelight LARRY,
happily sharing the very LAST

and most IMPORTANT page with EVERYONE!

(Well, perhaps not the VERY last page.)

"THaNKS for reading MY book. BUT...

Shhhhhh...

don't read it so loudly.

I'm not even meant to BE

on this page, you know."